Close Your Eyes

When nighty-night comes
We close our eyes
To dream our dreams
From Shushybye. . . .

Hold the cover of this book under a bright light for a minute and it will glow in the dark!

For my wife, Sandy,
who was the first child to ever visit Shushybye,
and to our children, David and Rachel,
two of Snoozles' favorite kids.
S.S.

For Skyler, Noah, and PT . . . my dream team.
F.C.

www.stmartins.com
Printed in China.
Library of Congress Cataloging-in-Publication Data is available
ISBN 13: 978-0-312-37381-8 ISBN 10: 0-312-37381-3
First published in the United States under the title: *Shushybye: Snoozles Saves the Night*
by The Shushybye Company. First Edition: Copyright © 2004 by The Shushybye Company.
First St. Martin's Press Edition: November 2007
10 9 8 7 6 5 4 3 2 1

Close Your Eyes

Written by Stephen Syatt • Illustrated by Frank Caruso

St. Martin's Press • New York

It was Shushybye time
for Leo and Leona.
Daddy turned out the light.
Mommy kissed the children good night.
"Now close your eyes," she whispered.
And she quietly closed the door.

But as soon as the door was closed,
Leo and Leona opened their eyes
and jumped out of their beds to play!

Every night, they stayed awake past their bedtime.
And because they were not sleeping,
they missed getting their special
Shushybye Dream Boxes with
their Shushybye dreams inside.

On top of a cloud, up high in the sky,
Is where you will find Shushybye.
The Shushies make dreams
To last the night through,
Then put them in Dream Boxes
And send them to you.

Snoozles was the Shushy who made special dreams for Leo and Leona. And Snoozles was worried. He wondered why their Dream Boxes were never opened.

Dozie and Zeez were Snoozles' best friends, and Dozie had an idea. "Let's visit the Shushybye King!" Dozie said. "He'll know what to do!"

Snoozles, Dozie, and Zeez climbed aboard the Shushybye Train. Conductor McCloud blew the great train's whistle and whisked the Shushies to the castle of the Shushybye King.

In no time at all, Snoozles
and his friends arrived at
the Shushybye Castle.
"How can I help you?"
asked the king.

Snoozles explained his problem.
"Leo and Leona keep missing their bedtime," he said.
"So, all their dreams are still inside their Dream Boxes!"

"You must visit Leo and Leona to find out why they keep missing their bedtime!"

With that, the Shushybye King circled his Dream Wand over Snoozles, who immediately fell fast asleep. "When you wake up, you'll be in Leo and Leona's room!" said the king.

Once again, it was Shushybye time for Leo and Leona.

Mommy noticed the sleeping Snoozles in the corner of their room. "Hmmm, I don't remember seeing that doll before!" she said, and she left them to fall asleep.

But Leo and Leona did not fall asleep!
"I wonder where this toy came from?" asked Leona.
Leo and Leona started to reach for Snoozles
just as he woke up!

"Where am I?" asked Snoozles.
"A talking toy!" cried Leona.
"My name is Leo," said her brother. "What's yours?"

"I'm Snoozles," he replied. "I'm a Shushy,
and I come from Shushybye!"
"Shushy what?" asked Leo and Leona.

"Shushybye is the land where your dreams are made," Snoozles explained.

"But when you stay up past your bedtime, you miss your Shushybye dreams!"

Leo and Leona ran downstairs to Mommy and Daddy.
"Come upstairs, quickly!" cried Leona.
"There's a Shushy in our room!" said Leo.

Mommy and Daddy could hardly believe what they saw.
"Mommy ... Daddy ... meet Snoozles," said Leo.
"Would you like to visit Shushybye?" Snoozles asked.
"I can show Leo and Leona where
their dreams come from!"

"What a wonderful idea," Mommy said. So Snoozles waved his magic Dream Wand. . . .

And in a flash, they were all in the castle of the Shushybye King!

"How nice to meet you!" exclaimed the king. "Come, let me show you around!"

Leo, Leona, Mommy, and Daddy stepped
into the Shushybye Dream Coach.
With a whoosh, they flew into the air.

The Shushybye King pointed out the sights of Shushybye. They saw the Rolling Hills of Nap Valley. . . .

They saw the tall palm trees of Yawn Island and the white sands of Snore Shore. Everywhere, busy Shushies were putting dreams into boxes for all the children.

Then they watched as Conductor McCloud loaded
Dream Boxes onto the Shushybye Train.

"So, Leo and Leona, what do you think?" asked the Shushybye King when their magical ride was over.
"I think we will close our eyes when we are told!" said Leo.
"We want to get our Shushybye dreams!" said Leona.

"But most of all," Mommy said, "we want to thank Snoozles.
He is our hero!"
"Indeed!" said the Shushybye King. "Snoozles, from this day on,
you shall be my special helper!"

Then the Shushybye King waved his Dream Wand, sending Mommy, Daddy, Leo, and Leona back home.

Once again, it was nighty-night time for Leo and Leona. And once again, Mommy came into their room to kiss them good night.

But this time, Leo and Leona
were fast asleep in their beds;
their eyes shut tight.

As Mommy turned out the light, she heard a
gentle toot as the Shushybye Train brought
Leo and Leona their Dream Boxes.

Nighty-night!

Shushybye Theme Song

Words and Music by Stephen Syatt

Every night the sun goes down,
The lights go out throughout your town.
That's the time to close your eyes,
'Cause soon you'll be in Shushybye.

Oh, my, my; Shushybye!
Oh, my, my; Shushybye!

There's a train that takes you to
A place where dreams are made for you.
Climb aboard; we'll ride the sky,
And soon you'll be in Shushybye.

Oh, my, my; Shushybye!
Oh, my, my; Shushybye!

All the dreams are there for you,
Dreams that last the whole night through.
So hold my hand and close your eyes;
We're on our way to Shushybye.

Oh, my, my; Shushybye!
Oh, my, my; Shushybye!